D0633851

Pete the Cat
Parents' Day Surprise

First Edition

AMAZON ORIGINAL

Pete the Cat

Parents' Day Surprise

HARPER FESTIVAL
An Imprint of HarperCollinsPublishers

Based on the Book Series by Kimberly and James Dean • Adapted by Anne Lamb from the Prime Video episode "Parents' Day Surprise" written by Lexie Kahanovitz

Pete and his friends are making pancakes for the Parents' Day Breakfast at school.
Pete's pancakes look like musical notes.

Grumpy covers his with extra syrup to attract flies. Emma makes her pancakes look like painters' palettes.

Everyone is having fun . . . except for Gustavo.

"What's wrong, Gus?" Pete asks.

"My mama was supposed to be here for the pancake breakfast," Gustavo says. "But she is in the military stationed far away, and a storm is preventing her from coming home."

Pete and his pals want to cheer Gus up. So they think of other ways for him
to send love to his mama on Parents' Day.
"I've got a great idea!" says Grumpy. "Let's make your mama a video!"

"She would love a video!" says Gustavo. "I've been thinking about writing a song for Mama. About how she's a pilot and how she does so much to protect us and how my love for her soars higher than the jet planes she flies. . . ."

Pete pulls out his guitar. "How about a music video?"
"That's a great idea!" says Gustavo. "But can you all help me?"
"Of course we will!" says Callie.
"I'm so lucky to have such amazing friends," Gus says.

Grumpy can't wait to get started.
"I'll direct!" he says. "We will set the video in outer space!"

Everyone has a job to do.
Callie collects costumes from the school theater.

Sally collects props to be the planets and stars.

Emma paints the background scenes.

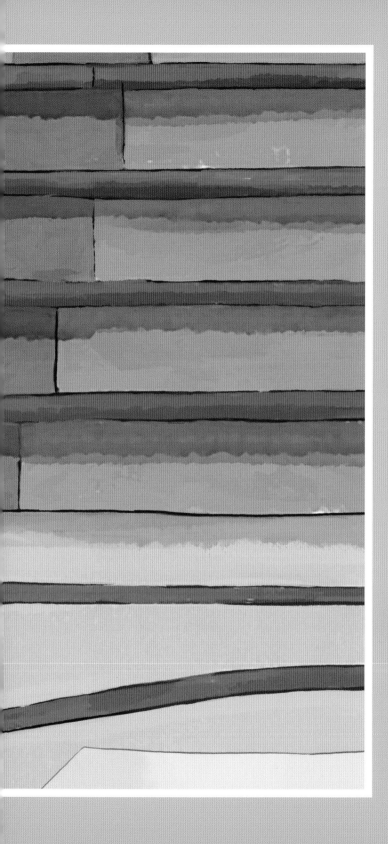

Pete practices his music while Gus writes the lyrics to the song. There is so much Gus wants to say, but it's not coming out quite right. "You are the pilot of my life, Mama, and . . . I am the copilot, and Papi is the . . . first officer? This is not what I want to say. . . ."

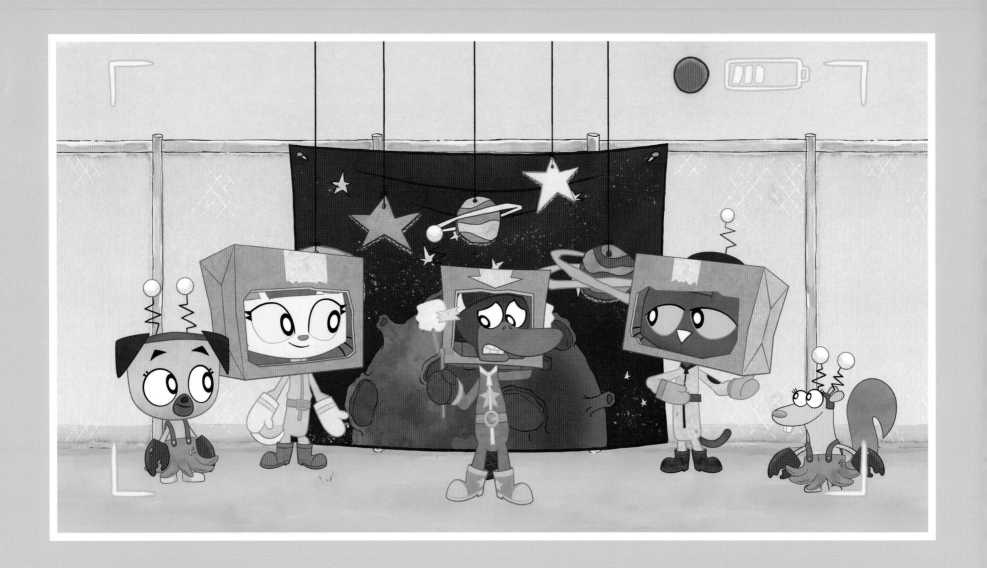

Before Gus knows it, everyone is ready to start filming the video.
"Action!" Grumpy shouts.
Gus tries to sing and dance, but he's too nervous. The words are
coming out all wrong.

"Cut!" says Grumpy.
"Let's just forget the video,"
Gus says as he walks away.

Pete finds his buddy on the playground.
"My mama is my hero," says Gus. "I just wish she were here for
Parents' Day so I could tell her that I'm so proud to be her son."

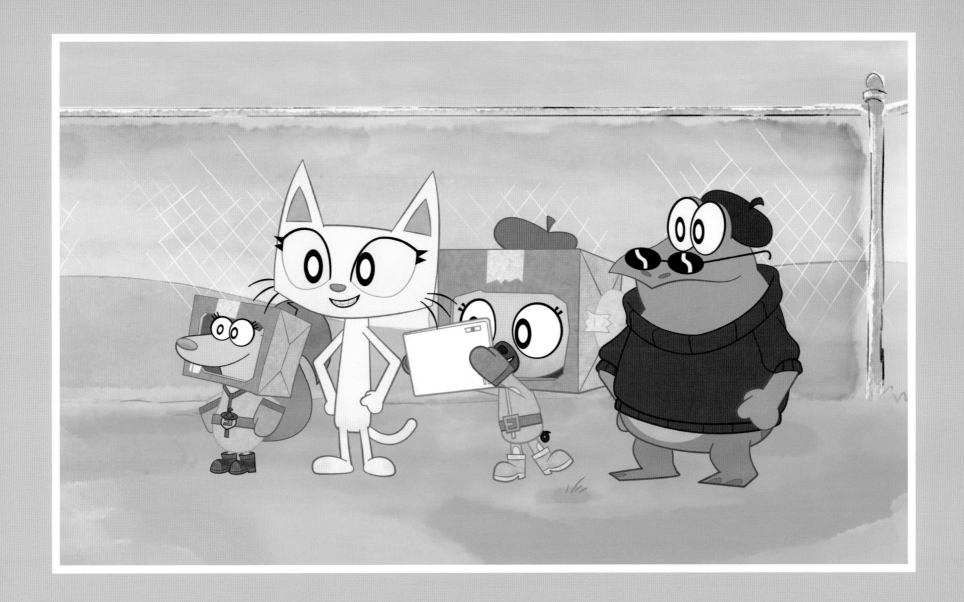

While Gus talks to Pete, his friends film all the nice things he says about his mama. They have a new secret plan that will cheer Gus up.

Later, at the Parents' Day Pancake Breakfast, Gus tells his papi about the video. "I tried to make a surprise for Mama," Gus says, "but it did not turn out well."

"That's okay," Papi says. "Your mama knows how much you love her."

Just then, Grumpy clears his throat.

"Excuse me. Can I have everyone's attention? I want to introduce a little film we made with Gus. . . ."

Gus realizes they're about to play the video for his mama. But how? He never finished it. . . .

Gus's friends worked together to finish the video as a surprise for Gus, and . . . it is awesome! Gus's song and video sound amazing!

"To keep us safe at home,
Mama jets across the sky,
and I want her to know
she makes my spirit fly. . . .

"I wish the jet you fly
would bring you home to me.
But I know you protect us all,
so we sing gratefully.

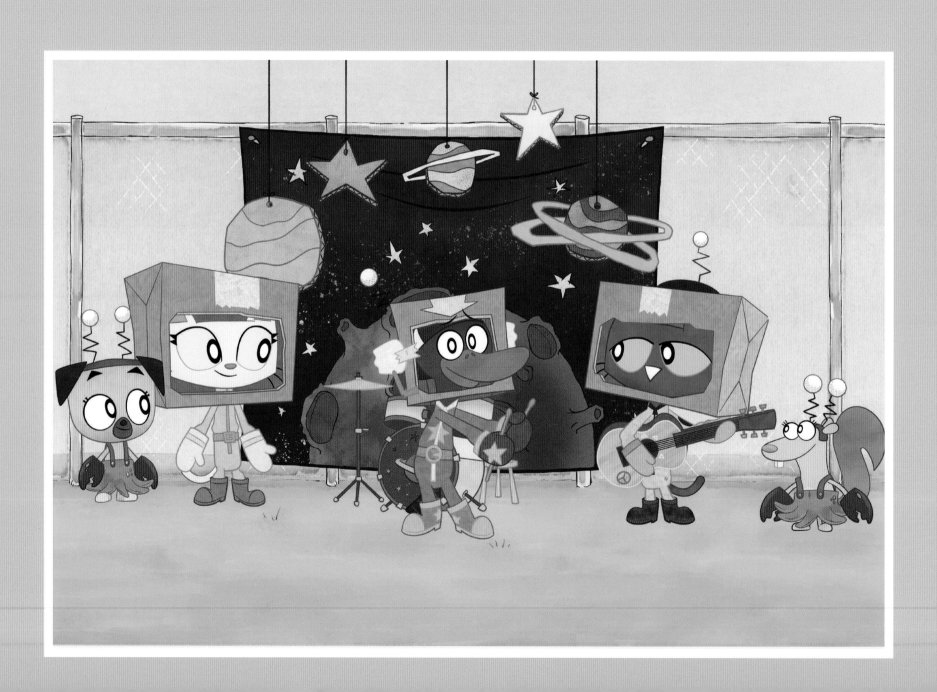

"For all the things you are,
and all the things you've done,
you are my shining star—
I'm so proud to be your son!

"This little tune I'm trying to croon
is completely true.
Like a red balloon, big as the moon,
that's my love for you!"

When the video ends, everyone at Parents' Day claps and cheers.
"That was amazing!" says Papi. "Your mama will be so surprised!"
"I am very excited for her to see it," says Gus. "Do you think she'll like it?"

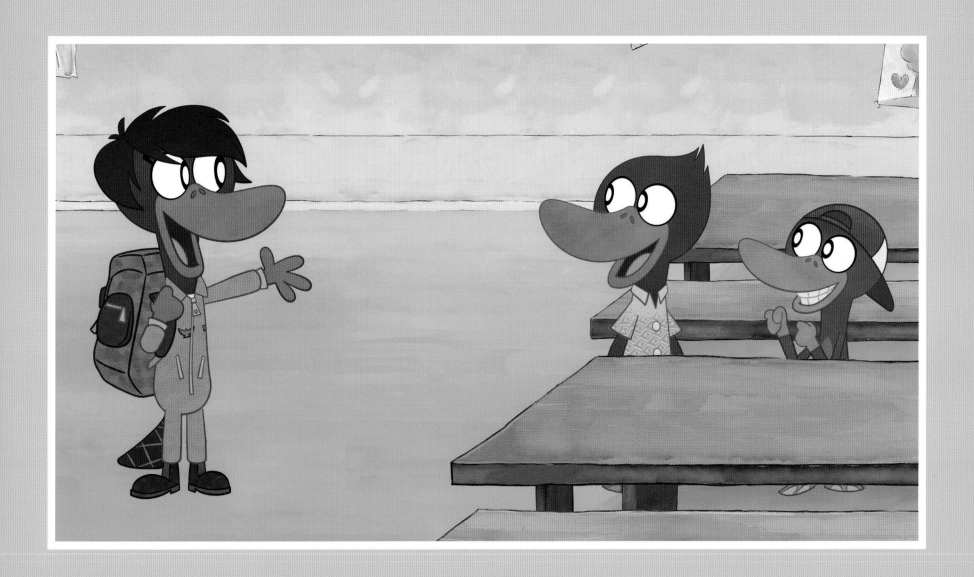

"Like it? I LOVE it, Gusti!" It's Gustavo's mama!

"Mama!" Gus gasps. "How can you be here? You were all the way around the world!"

"The storm cleared and I was able to make it after all!" Gus's mama gives him a big hug. "I wanted to surprise my two favorite guys," she says. "But what a lovely surprise for me."

Gustavo introduces his mama to his friends.
"Gustavo is so proud of you," Grumpy says.

"Well, I am very proud to be Gustavo's mama," Mama says,
pulling Gus and Papi in for a family hug.

Everyone sits down to enjoy the Parents' Day
pancakes. Gus can't stop smiling.
Pete says, "It always feels good to make
something for someone you love!"